Poodle draws doodles

Russell Punter

Illustrated by David Semple

Poodle draws doodles
of oodles of things...

from cooks, books and beetles
to spoons, brooms and kings.

She's having great fun,
sketching chickens and cows,

when she runs out of paper.

She looks down at her path.

"I'll chalk here!" she shouts.

"Then, after I've finished,
I'll wash it all out."

"I'll draw snakes eating cupcakes, with ice cream on top!"

Poodle gets so excited,
she forgets when to stop...

She chalks storks on Pug's birdbath,

and mice on his fruit.

Poor Pug finds a mole
on the sole of his boot.

"Stop that thief!" comes a shout,
"Save my painting, my dear!"

Poodle bounds into action.
She's had an idea.

An inviting escape route
takes no time to scrawl.

"Thank you, Poodle," pants Goose,
as the crook's led away.

Goose's business is booming,
thanks to Poodle's fine art.

Now she doodles on canvas
and Pug thinks that's smart!

About phonics

Phonics is a method of teaching reading used extensively in today's schools. At its heart is an emphasis on identifying the *sounds* of letters, or combinations of letters, that are then put together to make words. These sounds are known as phonemes.

Starting to read

Learning to read is an important milestone for any child. The process can begin well before children start to learn letters and put them together to read words. The sooner children can discover books and enjoy stories and language, the better they will be prepared for reading themselves, first with the help of an adult and then independently.

You can find out more about phonics on the Usborne Very First Reading website, **www.usborne.com/veryfirstreading** (US readers go to **www.veryfirstreading.com**). Click on the **Parents** tab at the top of the page, then scroll down and click on **About synthetic phonics**.

Phonemic awareness

An important early stage in pre-reading and early reading is developing phonemic awareness: that is, listening out for the sounds within words. Rhymes, rhyming stories and alliteration are excellent ways of encouraging phonemic awareness.

In this story, your child will soon identify the long *oo* sound, as in **poodle** and **doodle**. Look out, too, for rhymes such as **chalks** – **storks** and **scrawl** – **wall**.

Hearing your child read

If your child is reading a story to you, don't rush to correct mistakes, but be ready to prompt or guide if he or she is struggling. Above all, do give plenty of praise and encouragement.

Edited by Lesley Sims
Designed by Hope Reynolds

Reading consultants: Alison Kelly and Anne Washtell

First published in 2019 by Usborne Publishing Ltd., Usborne House, 83-85 Saffron Hill, London EC1N 8RT, England.
www.usborne.com Copyright © 2018 Usborne Publishing Ltd.